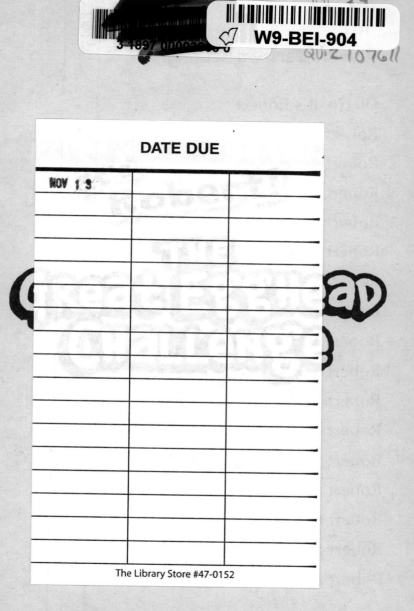

## Also by Barbara Seuling

# It's Robert!

# THE Great Egghead Challenge

## Barbara Seuling

### SCHOLASTIC INC.

**New York   Toronto   London   Auckland   Sydney
Mexico City   New Delhi   Hong Kong   Buenos Aires**

ISBN-13: 978-0-545-07193-2
ISBN-10: 0-545-07193-3

12   11   10   9   8   7   6   5   4   3          8   9   10 . 11   12   13/0

Printed in the U.S.A.      40

Previously published as *Robert and the Eggheads*

For James Bamberger.
—B. S.

# Contents

# Air

**R**obert's point broke. He took his stubby pencil with the chewed eraser over to the electric pencil sharpener at the side of the room. As he waited for the pencil to get sharp, Susanne Lee Rodgers walked up with two long new yellow pencils with perfect erasers on them. The points still looked sharp to Robert.

"You shouldn't chew your pencils, Robert. It's unsanitary," she said, flipping her hair off her shoulders.

Robert gritted his teeth. "Yeah," he managed to say.

Susanne Lee was always bossy, but she had been super annoying with her bossiness lately. She was still mad at him for having a party in Van Saun Park the same day she had her birthday party at The Pirate's Cove restaurant. He only did it because she had made a lot of people feel bad about being left out, especially Taylor, the new girl, who was deaf and already feeling left out. Robert couldn't help it that everyone at his party kept talking about what a good time they had, which made Susanne Lee even madder.

Robert went back to his seat with his pencil, now sharpened to a fine point.

Mrs. Bernthal tapped on her desk with a ruler. She walked over to the blackboard and wrote in big letters A I R.

"We are going to spend the next couple of weeks learning about how air is used to protect us and our valuables," she said. "On Monday you will need a blown egg, so please bring one to class as part of your homework."

Elizabeth Street raised her hand.

"What's a blown egg?" she asked, when Mrs. Bernthal called on her.

"It's an egg without its insides," said Mrs. Bernthal. "You make a pinhole at each end of the egg, then blow through one end and the egg comes out the other. The egg gets blown out without ruining the shell. Ask your parents to help you."

Robert hoped his mom had eggs in the refrigerator. You could never tell with her. Sometimes she got busy and didn't get around to or forgot the grocery shopping. He'd check when he got home.

"Oh. One more thing," Mrs. Bernthal said. "Be very careful bringing your egg to school. A blown egg will smash easily. See how clever you can be so that your egg is safe."

That shouldn't be so hard. Robert figured he'd wrap his in a sock or something.

# Spit

FFFFFFFFFFT! Huckleberry, Robert's big yellow lab, looked up at the sound. Robert blew as hard as he could into the hole at one end of the egg, but nothing came out the other end.

SSSPFFFFFFFFFFFT! Robert blew again. His cheeks were tired and there was spit all over the egg and running down his chin, but the egg was still inside.

Charlie walked into the kitchen and stopped short. "What are you doing?"

he asked. "Why are you spitting all over that egg?"

"I'm not," said Robert.

"Yeah, you are," said Charlie, looking at the mess on the table. "What's going on?"

"I'm not spitting, I'm blowing," said Robert. "I'm supposed to be blowing the egg out."

"Is there a hole there for it to come out?" said Charlie.

"Yeah. Mom helped me make a pin-hole. See?" He wiped off the egg and held it up to show Charlie.

"That's a pretty tiny hole for an egg to come through. You need a bigger hole." He moved toward the refrigerator, opened it, and helped himself to a juice drink.

Robert's mom walked in. "So how are you doing with that egg, Robbie?" she asked, cheerfully. "Sorry I had to leave you but I had to make a phone call." She looked around. "Oh my, I guess it's not going so well."

"Mom, that hole is too small," said Charlie.

Mrs. Dorfman picked up the egg with two fingers and rinsed it under the faucet. "You're right," she said. "I'm sorry, Rob. I'll fix it." She found the pin that she used to make the hole and poked lightly at the pinhole, making it a little bit bigger. "Here, try this." She handed the egg to Robert.

His jaws still ached from all the blowing he had done, but he tried again. Sure enough, the egg started to come out in a little yellow glop.

"Wait!" cried his mom, grabbing a small bowl from the sink drainer and whisking it over to him.

Robert blew the egg over the bowl. With a few more puffs, the egg came out.

Robert washed the egg again, making sure no egg or spit remained on it, and set it on the table to dry.

"What should I do with the bowl?" Robert asked his mom. His foot kicked the table leg as he turned in his chair.

"Watch out!" she cried. Charlie made a dive for it, but it was too late. The egg had rolled to the edge of the table and fallen to the floor. It was smashed. Huckleberry got up and walked over to it, sniffing. He licked it up, shell and all.

"Oh, what a shame! Well, you'll just have to do it again," said his mom, handing him another egg. "When you finish, put the bowl in the fridge. I'll scramble the eggs for Huckleberry in the morning,"

"Remind me not to have eggs for breakfast," said Charlie. "I prefer mine without spit."

# Faces

Getting his egg to school was not easy. Wrapping it in a sock wouldn't work. If he stuffed it into his backpack, his books would crush the egg right through the sock. He couldn't put it in his pocket. How could he carry it?

Robert looked everywhere for a box. A shoe box was too big. A jewelry box was too small. Desperate, he even looked in the refrigerator. There were containers of leftover Chinese food.

One of those might work.

He put the leftover Chinese food in a bowl, then washed out the container and dried it with a paper towel. This was good. The container even had a little handle.

Paul Felcher, Robert's best friend, was waiting on his corner for Robert, as usual. They never took the school bus unless there was an emergency.

"Why are you bringing Chinese food to school?" asked Paul. "Is that your lunch?"

"No," said Robert. "It's my egg for our project."

As they walked, Robert told Paul about the mess he had made blowing his egg.

"Yeah," said Paul, holding up his egg

inside a plastic bag. "I know what you mean. Nick got hold of the first egg I was about to blow and thought it was a ball so he threw it." Nick was Paul's little brother.

"Oh no!" said Robert. "Did he?"

"Yup. He did. And I caught it. Yuck. It was gross. I had egg dripping off me everywhere."

Robert laughed. "I guess my mess wasn't so bad then," he said.

"What do you suppose we're going to do with our eggs?" said Paul.

"I don't know. Some kind of experiment, I bet."

"I hope we don't have to blow any more," said Paul.

"Yeah," Robert agreed. "My cheeks will burst."

That morning, Mrs. Bernthal explained how they were going to use their eggs in a science experiment.

Paul leaned over and whispered, "You were right!"

Robert nodded, pleased.

"Your egg is going to be part of an interesting experiment," said Mrs. Bernthal, "so take good care of it."

The children giggled.

"You may even decorate it in some way," she continued. "Put your name on it, make a face, whatever. Your job will be to protect your egg to the best of your ability. You want no harm to come to it."

"I thought we were studying air, not eggs," Lester Willis called out.

"Raise your hand when you have

something to say, Lester," said Mrs. Bernthal. "You will soon see how air plays a big part in your experiment."

The children, buzzing now, got busy, taking out pencils and markers.

Robert made a face on his. It was Huckleberry, his dog. Paul drew a man's face on his. He called it Steve, the astronaut. The idea spread quickly around the classroom. Taylor Jerome made a face on hers and drew on two red hearing aids, just like the ones she wore.

Lester Willis had everyone laughing. He had made his with long eyelashes and big red lips. "It's Juliet," he said. "And I'm Romeo." He kissed his egg with a big, loud, slurping sound. Lester was pretty funny sometimes.

Susanne Lee just sucked her teeth

and said, "He's pitiful," loud enough so that Lester could hear it. Lester didn't seem to care. He was having fun.

Susanne Lee refused to make a face on her egg. She just wrote her name across it: SUSANNE LEE. Robert thought Susanne Lee would be a lot nicer if she could just have fun once in a while.

Robert was drawing whiskers on Huckleberry's face when Mrs. Bernthal made her announcement.

Mrs. Bernthal walked to the chalkboard where she had written the word AIR. "This experiment," she said, "is to learn how to package your egg, using air to protect it. We will test your packages by dropping them from different heights. Your egg should survive the fall without breaking."

This was going to be interesting. Robert still didn't know how air figured into it, but he figured he'd learn pretty soon.

"You are going to work with a partner for the next few days as we do our experiment." She read from a piece of paper. "Emily and Joey, you are partners. Lucy and Kevin, Andy and Vanessa, Maggie and Brian. . . ." She went down the list. Robert couldn't believe it when he heard her say, "Robert and Susanne Lee."

He groaned and slouched down in his chair.

# Partners

Robert had always liked working with a partner when that partner was Paul. Then it was fun and they laughed a lot. He didn't think he was going to laugh a lot with Susanne Lee.

Paul leaned over. "Bummer," he said.

Robert nodded in agreement. He looked over at Susanne Lee. She was smiling that bossy smile of hers, like she was already in charge. Robert slid down in his chair and stared at his egg.

"Sorry, Huck," he whispered to his egg.

"When you work with your partner," said Mrs. Bernthal, "you can change your seat. Try it now, and show your egg to your partner."

Robert moved to Table Number Three, where Susanne Lee sat.

"Hi," said Robert. "This is Huckleberry. He's a dog."

Susanne Lee snorted as though a dog was a stupid thing to draw on an egg. "It's not a dog. It's an egg," she said. Her egg lay on the table plain, with no face.

Robert felt really stupid.

He was relieved when they went back to their own seats. He tried to forget about Susanne Lee during their writing session. He had trouble with spelling, but he liked to write stories. Mrs. Bernthal told them to write about someone they knew, so he wrote about Susanne Lee as The Princess Who Wouldn't Smile. He was writing about everyone in the kingdom trying to get the princess to smile, tickling her with feathers, bringing in clowns and jugglers, and still she wouldn't smile. In the end, they found out she ate lemons for breakfast. They threw away all the lemons in the kingdom, and she finally smiled.

By the time they went to lunch, he had almost forgotten about the egg project. Then Mrs. Bernthal reminded them of it again before the three o'clock bell rang.

"Children," said Mrs. Bernthal, "for homework tomorrow I'd like you to bring in materials that you can use to protect your egg if it falls or is handled roughly."

Robert tucked his books into his backpack. His egg lay on the table.

"And before you leave today," continued Mrs. Bernthal, "put your eggs away carefully. We will work with them again tomorrow."

Robert looked around. He walked around the room with his egg in his hand. He was surprised that he felt protective about it. He came to the windowsill where several plants were lined up. The amaryllis was his favorite. He had seen it bloom into a big beautiful red flower, but after the flower was gone it was just a tall thick stem with lots of long leaves around it.

It was in a big pot with a lot of soil. He touched the soil. It was slightly damp from the last watering. His finger left a small depression in the soil. He pressed harder. He pressed until he had made a deep enough depression for his egg. He placed the egg in the soil.

"Very clever," Susanne Lee said, coming up behind him. She followed his example and put hers in the soil of the plant next to the amaryllis.

Robert couldn't believe it. Susanne Lee had paid him a compliment.

# In-su-lation

Robert searched the house for something to put his egg in that would keep it from breaking.

"Mom," he said, walking into her little upstairs office, "do you have anything I can wrap my egg in so it won't get smashed?"

Robert's mom stopped typing at her computer and thought. She reached into a desk drawer and pulled out an envelope. "This is padded," she said, looking in, "but I think it would squoosh an egg."

"Okay. Thanks anyway," said Robert, and went downstairs to ask his dad, who was watching TV. Charlie was sprawled on the sofa, eating popcorn. A commercial was on, so Robert felt safe interrupting.

"Dad," he said, "I have to make sure my egg doesn't break. Do you know anything I can use?"

"Ho!" said Charlie, breaking in. "Is that the egg you spit on?"

"I didn't spit on it," said Robert. He turned back to his father. "Do you, Dad?"

Robert's dad looked interested. "You're talking about insulation, right?"

"No. Maybe. I don't know. It's a science experiment about air. I have to put my egg in something to keep it from breaking. What's insulation?"

"Get the dictionary."

He should have known it wouldn't be that easy to ask his dad for help. Robert went over to the bookcase and pulled out the dictionary. He brought it to the coffee table and began to look up the word.

"I - N -" he said, leafing through the pages.

"I-N-S-U-L-A-T-E," added his father.

At least his dad wasn't going to make him work at spelling the word himself. He found the word. "In-su-late," he read. "1. To set apart; de- de-tach from the rest; i-so-late." He looked up to see if this was right.

"Go on," his dad said.

Robert continued, sounding out the words. "2. To sep-a-rate or cover with a non-con-duct-ing ma- mat- mat-er-i-al in order to pre-vent the passage or leak-age of electri-ci-ty, heat, or sound." He took a breath, not understanding a word of what he had just read.

Robert's dad explained it. "That means," he said, "that something—like air—is used to keep something else out—like a hard knock."

Why did they use all those words to say something so simple? How could anyone understand it? His dad must be a genius.

"What you need," said his dad, "is something to surround your egg to keep it from being hurt by anything that might break it."

"Like if it falls?" asked Robert.

"Yes."

"What if I put it in a box?" asked Robert.

"It could roll around in the box and hit the sides, and that could break it. But, if you crumpled up newspapers and put them all around your egg, all the air that's trapped in the folds of the newspaper would protect it."

Robert considered that. It made sense. There were plenty of newspapers around the house.

"You can even use this," said Mr. Dorfman, reaching over to the bowl in Charlie's lap and grabbing a handful of popcorn.

"Hey!" said Charlie, pulling the bowl back.

Popcorn! Robert wondered what Susanne Lee would think about that.

"But you'd need plenty of it, and you'd have to fill up a box much bigger than the egg, then put the egg deep in the center of it."

Robert didn't have that big a box or that much popcorn, with Charlie wolfing it down so fast. So even though it was a good idea, he decided the newspaper idea seemed to be the best bet.

# The Best Packing Ever

**S**ure enough, the next day Mrs. Bernthal explained all about how air is used as a shock absorber.

Robert felt good that he already knew something about that. His dad hadn't called it that, but it was the same thing.

"You know the bicycle helmets you wear?" asked Mrs. Bernthal. "And football helmets? There is a layer of air between the part that fits on your head and the hard outer shell. The air locked between the two layers is what keeps your head from getting hurt when you fall."

"In-su-la-tion," Robert whispered out loud as he doodled in his notebook.

"Yes, Robert. Insulation." She smiled at him before turning around to write it out on the chalkboard. "That's a big word that you can all look up."

Robert glanced over at Susanne Lee. Sure enough, she was looking his way. She even had a little smile on her face. Surely, he couldn't have impressed her! He slunk down in his chair and continued to doodle.

Kids had brought in all kinds of materials to protect their eggs. Emily Asher had a shopping bag full of plastic peanuts that had come with a new DVD player. Lucy Ritts brought in the cardboard container from her mom's bath powder. It still smelled like flowers. Susanne Lee brought in a mayonnaise jar filled nearly to the top with water. Her egg floated in the space at the top. Lester brought in bubble wrap and kept popping the bubbles. With all the crinkling and squooshing and popping, Mrs. Bernthal had to tap her ruler several times to get them quiet.

"You all seem to have the idea. Now I want you to think like inventors. Go to work and put your egg in a protective package. Remember what I told you about how air acts as a shock absorber. Your egg will have to withstand a lot of punishment."

"You mean like falling off the table?"

"Yes, like falling off the table—and worse."

"Like getting sat on?"

"Yes, that's a good example, too."

Robert wasn't sure his egg would survive getting sat on, no matter how much crumpled newspaper he used, especially if the person who sat on it was big, like Lester.

Susanne Lee was worried, too. "We need something that's foolproof," she said, with determination in her eyes.

"Take your time," said Mrs. Bernthal, "and think about it carefully. Tomorrow we're going to drop the eggs on the hard floor."

There was a gasp from the class.

"But our eggs will break!" said Melissa Thurm.

"That's just the point," said Mrs. Bernthal. It's your job to see that they don't break. Remember that air can absorb shock. Use air in some way you can think of to keep your egg intact through some clever device or package."

Mrs. Bernthal always used grown-up language with them, but they always understood her.

"Think of air bags in cars, shoulder pads that football players wear, and the sneakers you all wear. Air is a part of all those things, acting as a shock absorber. Work together and come up with the best package possible. I'm going to mark you as a team for this project."

Susanne Lee looked at the jar of water in front of her. "This will never work," she said miserably.

Robert had thought that was a cool way to carry an egg, too, until now, but Susanne Lee couldn't drop a jar. It would break.

"What if you put your egg and water in a plastic container instead of a glass jar?" he suggested, trying to be helpful.

Susanne Lee actually thought about it. "I can try it, but I think even plastic would break if it's dropped. Or the lid would pop off. I may have to think of something else."

"What about this?" he asked, looking at his own egg in its nest of crumpled newspaper.

"I don't know. Newspaper works for just bumps and taps. But I don't think it will work falling on the hard floor.

Robert, we have some work to do."

That "we" sounded scary to Robert. How could he come up with something even Susanne Lee couldn't think of?

"Think hard, Robert." Now she was using her bossy voice. "I want ours to be the best packaging ever. We've got to come up with something nobody else has thought of."

Robert swallowed hard. What could they possibly think of that nobody else had thought of before? He didn't even know how to begin.

# Eggheads

**R**obert and Paul walked home to Robert's house, planning to do their homework together. Nobody was home except for Huckleberry, who met them at the door, wagging his tail so hard it looked like it would wag right off.

They dropped their backpacks beside the umbrella stand and reached down to pat Huckleberry and scratch behind the big dog's ears. Huckleberry immediately rolled over, and Robert knelt down beside him to give him a belly rub.

"Come on, Huck," he said, getting up. "Let's go play." Paul followed as they went out to the backyard for a game of catch. Huck ran all over the yard, fetching the ball and bringing it back to Robert to throw it again. He never got tired of this game, unless he saw a squirrel. Then Huck would race after the squirrel, the squirrel would flee up the tree, and Huck would stand at the base of the tree barking and whining and waiting for the squirrel to come down, which it never did.

While Huck ran back and forth fetching the ball, Robert said, "Do you have your egg package done?" Paul had showed Robert his package while he was making it. It was a cage for the egg made out of pipe cleaners.

"Not yet," said Paul. "It needs something else. I'll work on it some more tonight."

"Me too," said Robert.

"I thought yours was ready."

"I thought it was, but Susanne Lee thinks we need something better."

"That sounds like Susanne Lee. She has to do it better than anyone else," said Paul. "What are you going to do?"

"That's just it. I don't know. All we came up with so far is newspapers and a jar of water."

"Yeah," said Paul, scratching his head. "The jar is a problem."

"Exactly," said Robert. "I mean, eggsactly."

Paul laughed. "I told my mom about our eggheads, and she told me 'egghead' is a word used for a smart person."

"Really?" asked Robert. "You mean Mrs. Bernthal is an egghead?"

"No. It's not really a compliment," said Paul.

"Oh, I get it," said Robert. "It's some-one who thinks they're smarter than everybody, right?"

"Right."

Robert stopped suddenly. "Wait!" he said.

"What?"

"I'm working with one. Susanne Lee is definitely an egghead!" They fell onto the grass, laughing. Huck had treed a squirrel but left his post at the base of the tree and climbed on top of them, acting like this was an even better game.

They went inside to start on their homework.

"Paul, do you want to eat with us tonight?" asked Robert's mom, as they passed by the kitchen.

"Um, I don't know, Mrs. Dorfman. I have to ask my mom." He looked at Robert helplessly.

Robert's mom was not a great cook, so unless dinner was takeout from the Happy Wok Chinese restaurant, chances were, dinner would be a lot better over at the Felchers' house.

"What are we having for dinner, Mom?" Robert asked, to give Paul a chance to think.

"Chinese."

Paul brightened. "Okay, I'll call my mom." He picked up the telephone, and Robert heard him say, "Thanks, Mom," as he hung up.

"I can stay," he said. He and Robert did a high five.

"Great," said Robert's mom. "I'll call you when it's time to wash up."

They thumped up the stairs, grinning.

Dinner dishes had been cleared, and Robert's mom brought out dessert— red Jell-O with fruit pieces floating in it. As Robert dug his spoon into the shimmery stuff, he stopped short.

"Mom?" he said.

"Yes, Robbie?"

"How did you get the fruit into the Jell-O?"

"Oh, that?" said his mom. "You wait until the Jell-O is almost set. Then you add the fruit. It's easy. I'll show you next time."

"Can you show me tonight?" asked Robert.

"Tonight?" she said. "You want more Jell-O tonight?"

"Not to eat. It's for a science experiment. Can you?"

"Well, sure," his mom answered. "I don't see why not."

"Great."

Robert felt a little wave of pleasure creep over him.

Paul, sitting next to him, scooped out the last of his dessert and licked his spoon. "Why do you want to make Jell-O?" he asked.

"Because Susanne Lee wants us to be the best," he said.

"Since when do you care what Susanne Lee wants?"

That was a good question. Usually, Susanne Lee and her bossy ways just bothered him. This time, he was excited by her determination to be successful.

He shrugged. "I don't know. Maybe I'm turning into an egghead, too."

They both cracked up and had to be excused from the table.

# In Shock

This was Egg Drop Day. Everyone had their egghead in some kind of protective container.

Kristi Mills had brought in a box full of plastic peanuts, and she and Paul, her partner, were putting both their ideas together. Their egg was in an elaborate pipe cleaner cage, and the cage was nestled in a bed of a gazillion plastic peanuts in a cardboard box. From the picture on the box, it looked like it had once held a coffeemaker.

Robert watched as Susanne Lee took a plastic zipper-lock bag out of her backpack. It was filled with water and had an egg in it.

"What's that?" asked Robert.

"The hard plastic containers didn't work; I tried some, and their lids popped off. I thought this might work," she answered, holding it up. "Oops!" Susanne Lee held her other hand under the bag. "It's leaking."

Robert ran to get paper towels from the supply cabinet to help sop up the water. Susanne Lee dumped her backpack out on the table. Her notebook was soaking wet. She groaned.

"I guess that didn't work," she said, finally. Mrs. Bernthal handed her the pass, and Susanne Lee left the room with her leaking bag. She was probably going to the girls' room, so Robert couldn't follow her.

Susanne Lee didn't look happy when she came back. "We'll never win the egg drop now," she complained.

"Wait," said Robert. "I have something to show you."

Susanne Lee looked like she was only slightly interested in whatever Robert had to show her.

Robert thought of his egghead discussion with Paul yesterday. He reached into his backpack and took out a small tomato sauce can with aluminum foil over the top. He took off the foil and showed it to Susanne Lee. She stared into the can.

"It's Jell-O," said Robert. There was Robert's egg, buried in the red stuff, looking like it was floating.

Susanne Lee's mouth dropped open. "Robert!" she exclaimed, her eyes wide. "You're so smart. Why didn't I think of that?"

Robert had no answer for that. He was in shock from hearing Susanne Lee call him "smart." No one had ever called him that before.

"Do you realize what this means?" Susanne Lee squealed. Robert thought she might grab him, and he stepped back.

"Wha-what?" he stammered.

"It means we have a chance to win, you goose!" she sputtered.

"Really?" Robert wasn't used to all

this excitement over something he had done.

"Well, not win, exactly," said Susanne Lee. "But our egg won't break when it's dropped. I'm practically sure of it!"

Robert smiled. "I guess," he answered. That was the point, wasn't it? He didn't see anything extraordinary about what he'd done, but there was definitely a warm feeling inside, knowing Susanne Lee thought he was smart.

After recess, Mrs. Bernthal tapped her desk for order. The class quieted down.

"It's time for our Egg Drop," she said. Robert felt a rush.

One by one, Mrs. Bernthal called up the teams.

Emily Asher and Joey Rizzo came up

with a cereal box.

"How did you protect your egg?" asked Mrs. Bernthal.

"We wrapped it in tissue paper, then packed it in a small box and then in the cereal box with crumpled newspaper," said Emily.

"Okay. Here we go." Mrs. Bernthal held it up high above her head with both hands and counted "One . . . two . . . three . . ." and let it drop.

Brian scrambled to open the box. He pulled the newspaper out. Their egg was okay! The children applauded.

"Okay," said Mrs. Bernthal. "You passed the first test."

Lucy and Kevin went up next. Their egg was wrapped in a quilted baby blanket. It survived the drop, too.

Andy Liskin and Maggie Lee used a cardboard egg carton, and their egg shattered.

"Oh no!" cried Maggie. Andy picked up the carton, and they went back to their seats.

Matt Blakey had squeezed a small egg into a cardboard toilet paper tube. It survived a bit of batting around but didn't make it through the drop.

When Robert and Susanne Lee went up, Robert held his breath as Mrs. Bernthal dropped their can. The aluminum cover fell off, but the Jell-O stayed inside and the egg was okay.

"Yes!" shouted Robert.

Susanne Lee smiled, but Robert could tell she was thinking: Would it make it through the next test? Actually, he was thinking that, too.

"Line up," called Mrs. Bernthal, after all the teams had dropped their eggs. "We're going to the gymnasium." Robert carried their egghead carefully.

Mrs. Bernthal carried a large cardboard box. In the auditorium, she had the class sit in the first two rows and placed the box on the floor in front of the auditorium, below the stage. Then she climbed a few stairs to the stage.

"You will come up two at a time, in teams. I will drop your egg from the stage into the box. If your egg survives, you have passed the second test."

Yikes. Robert wondered if their egghead could survive such a tough test.

Team by team, the class showed its best efforts. At the end, there were seven teams left with unsmashed eggs. Robert and Susanne were one of the seven teams. So were Paul and Kristi Mills.

"Tonight you will have one more chance to make sure your packaging is the best," said Mrs. Bernthal, "because tomorrow your egghead will be dropped from the first floor window. Any team whose egghead survives this last drop will receive a 'Bright Idea' pin." She held up a cool pin with a light bulb that flashed on and off. Robert wanted that pin. "So good luck to you, and may the best team win," said Mrs. Bernthal.

Robert and Susanne stared at each other. Their Jell-O egghead would never survive being dropped out of a window!

# A Weird Plan

"**M**om, can we get Chinese food tonight?" Robert asked. "I need one of those take-out containers for my project."

"Well," Robert's mom said, "I was going to make a meatloaf. . . ."

"No! . . ." Robert began, but Charlie interrupted.

"Yeah, Mom. Let's do take-out and help Robert with his project," said Charlie. Everyone preferred dinner from a restaurant to Robert's mom's cooking.

"Well, okay," she said.

When the order came, and they opened the containers, Robert yelled "STOP!" before anyone could plunge a fork into the lo mein, which was mostly noodles. He grabbed the container. "Can I have this?"

"Yes, Robert, as soon as we're done. I'll wash it and give it to you. Now let's eat."

"No!" shouted Robert. Then he apologized. "I'm sorry. It's just . . . I mean . . . I want to use the whole thing."

"With the noodles?" said Charlie.

"Yes," said Robert quickly, although now he was a bit embarrassed by his outburst. He had to explain.

"Susanne Lee and I have to win when our egg is dropped out a window tomorrow. The tomato sauce can with the Jell-O isn't enough to protect it. We have to wrap it so it really can't break!"

"Since when are you such a science freak?" asked Charlie.

Robert ignored him. Charlie liked to tease him.

"And how are the noodles going to help?" asked his mom.

Robert continued. "We'll put the can inside the take-out container and pack noodles all around it."

"That's a weird plan," said Charlie.

"No, it's actually a good idea!" said Robert's dad. "Robert has the right concept of what absorbs shock."

Robert didn't know what "concept"

meant, but it sounded like a good thing.

"You can't be serious," said Robert's mom. "He can't take lo mein to school for his project!"

"Well, lo mein is a little messy, but what about rice?" Robert's dad said. "It's not as messy, and we always have plenty left over. Besides, there's lots more air between the grains of rice than around the noodles."

Robert looked gratefully at his dad. He had never seen his dad get so excited about something he did for school before.

Charlie, meanwhile, reached for the sesame chicken. "I hope no one needs this for a school project," he joked.

At last, everyone was convinced that

Robert's idea might work, and after dinner they watched as he packed the rice carefully around the tomato sauce can in the take-out carton.

Robert called Susanne Lee and told her what he had done. She sounded excited. "That's great, Robert," she said. "I have something, too, and now I think we can put our two ideas together and be the best."

"What is it?" he asked.

"Meet me tomorrow morning before the bell rings and I'll show you."

When he hung up the phone, Robert wasn't sure who he was anymore. Had he morphed into some other person? He was not used to having Susanne Lee talk to him like he actually had a brain.

# The "Bright Idea" Pin

**R**obert ran up to Paul's corner out of breath. "C'mon," he panted. "I have to meet Susanne Lee before school starts."

"Why?" Paul asked, hurrying to keep up. "Why are you suddenly interested in Susanne Lee?"

"I'm not," said Robert. It was just the excitement of getting their project to work. Wasn't it?

"It's our egg package," he told Paul.

"We both have these great ideas, and Susanne Lee wants to combine them for today's experiment. I can't wait to see what she came up with."

He explained about the Chinese food container and the discussion last night at the dinner table about lo mein noodles and leftover rice.

"I'm glad I didn't have to mess with that," Paul said. "I just made more pipe cleaner cages, each one bigger than the one before."

"Wow," said Robert. "That sounds cool, too." Leave it to Paul to come up with something as clever as the pipe cleaner cages for his egg. Nobody else in a gazillion years would think of anything like that. That's why Paul would probably be an astronaut some day. He was not only an artist. He was brilliant.

At the school yard, Susanne Lee sat on the step outside the door with her backpack at her feet.

"So where is it?" asked Robert.

"Right there," said Susanne Lee, pointing to her backpack.

"What's in there?"

"No, not in it. That's it. The backpack."

"What do you mean?" Robert pulled out the Chinese take-out container from his own backpack.

"That's cool," said Susanne Lee. "Put it inside the backpack. I've stuffed it with newspaper, so squoosh the paper down around the take-out box. Try to keep the box in the center."

Talk about brilliant! Robert had never

been around so many smart people in one day. It made his neck itch!

The experiment did not take place until late morning. Robert had to struggle through spelling and math and a reading quiz before he could concentrate on the Egg Drop project again.

At last Mrs. Bernthal announced they were going to assemble in the principal's office. Mr. Lipkin was going to let them use his window for their launch pad.

"Right outside, underneath Mr. Lipkin's window, is a concrete sidewalk, so this will be a good test of your packing skills," she told them. "After each drop, you will go down into the front yard to pick up your package and bring it back up to our classroom. Once we're all back together, we'll open them."

The tension was really great now. Emily and Joey went first. Then Andy and Vanessa. Then Robert and Susanne Lee.

As soon as the backpack was dropped, they ran like the wind out the door and to the front yard to retrieve it. They each held on to a part of the backpack as they ran back up to the classroom. Robert stared at the backpack. The suspense was going to kill him.

Finally, the room filled up and everyone was back in their project seats. Robert sat at Susanne Lee's table, the backpack there between them. It took a lot of control for Robert not to tear into it to see if their egg was okay.

One by one, the teams opened their

packages and held up their eggs to see.

"Emily and Brian, you're next," said Mrs. Bernthal. Emily tore open the cereal box, and Brian unwrapped the bubble wrap inside it. When they got to their egg, it was fine.

"Yay!" yelled Vanessa. Everyone applauded.

Lucy and Kevin Kransky were disappointed when their egg came out smashed.

Paul and Kristi went next. Kristi opened the big cardboard box. Paul pulled out the newspaper. Kristi lifted out the pipe cleaner construction and handed it to Paul. One by one, Paul undid the pipe cleaners from each other. When he finally got to the last little cage around the egg, he handed it to Kristi. Kristi took the cage apart and held up the egg. It was perfect!

"Very good, Kristi and Paul," said Mrs. Bernthal, to the applause of the children. "Now, Susanne Lee and Robert."

At last!

They both reached for the backpack at once. Susanne Lee unzipped it. Robert pulled out newspaper left and right until he got to the Chinese takeout container. Susanne Lee opened it and turned it over on the table. Out came the tomato sauce can, along with a lot of rice. Robert took the can and lifted the foil. They looked into the Jell-O, and there was their egg, with the Huckleberry face, staring back at them, in perfect shape.

"Hurray!" someone shouted. It sounded

like Lester. The class applauded.

"You have certainly worked out a clever plan," said Mrs. Bernthal.

As they went back to their seats, Susanne Lee whispered to Robert, "Thanks. This was really fun."

Robert gulped and resisted the urge to scratch his neck where it itched so badly.

"Yeah," he said. "It was."

In the end, three teams won "Bright Idea" pins, with the light bulbs on them from Mrs. Bernthal.

As they walked home from school that afternoon, Robert and Paul displayed their flashing light bulb pins on their jackets.

"So now we're eggheads, too," said Paul.

"Oh no!" said Robert, pretending to be dying a terrible death. "Not that!"

He and Paul cracked up.

"You know the best part of this?" said Paul.

"What?" asked Robert.

"It's over!" said Paul. And that cracked them up all over again.

**BARBARA SEULING** is a well-known author of fiction and nonfiction books for children, including several books about Robert. She divides her time between New York City and Vermont.

**Read about Robert's very bad day in**

# The Triple Rotten Day.

Robert thumped down the stairs and into the kitchen. He let Huckleberry out the door into the backyard.

"Good morning, Rob," said his mom.

"Good morning," he answered, digging the scoop into the dog food bag to fill Huckleberry's bowl. Robert watched his brother slug down a glass of orange juice, then jump up to leave. When Robert got to the table, he reached for the container. He poured, but nothing came out.

"Is there any more orange juice?" he asked.

"I'm afraid not," said his mom. "I'll

put it on the shopping list."

She got up and wrote something on a pad on the refrigerator door, with a pencil that hung from it. "Would you like some grapefruit juice?" she asked.

Robert slumped in his chair. "No, thanks." He hated grapefruit juice. He chewed the edges of a toaster tart around and around until it was just the soft middle. Then he ate that part last, washing it down with milk.

Robert's mom put a brown paper bag next to his plate. "Don't forget your lunch," she reminded him.

"Thanks," he answered, slipping off the chair and into his jacket. He stuffed the lunch bag into his backpack and kissed his mom good-bye.

"See you later," she said. "Have a good day."

"Thanks," said Robert again, slinging the backpack over his shoulder. He waved a good-bye behind him as he ran down the path. He felt grumpy, but he knew things would get better once he met Paul. Every morning Paul Felcher, his best friend, waited for Robert on Paul's corner and they walked to school together. They only took the bus if the weather was bad.

Could it be? Paul wasn't there. But Paul was always there. Unless . . . that must be it. The last time Paul wasn't there was when he was out sick.

Robert dragged his feet, walking the long blocks to school alone. It was as though his sneakers had cement in them.

In the classroom, Robert put his backpack in his space at Table Four, where he sat with Vanessa Nicolini next to him and Paul across from him. Except today. Paul's chair was empty. Being in Mrs. Bernthal's classroom could usually cheer Robert up, but today he was worried.